My Purple Scented Novel

Ian McEwan

My Purple Scented Novel

VINTAGE

1 3 5 7 9 10 8 6 4 2

Vintage
20 Vauxhall Bridge Road,
London SW1V 2SA

Vintage is part of the Penguin Random House group of companies whose addresses can be found at global.penguinrandomhouse.com.

This story was inspired by 'L'image volée', an exhibition project by Thomas Demand which opened at Fondazione Prada in Milan and was published by the *New Yorker* in March 2016

First published by Vintage in 2018

penguin.co.uk/vintage

A CIP catalogue record for this book is available from the British Library

ISBN 9781784709389

Typeset in 12.75/18 pt Centaur MT Pro
by Integra Software Services Pvt. Ltd, Pondicherry

Printed and bound in Great Britain by Clays Ltd, St Ives plc

Penguin Random House is committed to a sustainable future for our business, our readers and our planet. This book is made from Forest Stewardship Council® certified paper.

My Purple Scented Novel

YOU WILL HAVE HEARD OF MY FRIEND the once celebrated novelist Jocelyn Tarbet, but I suspect his memory is beginning to fade. Time can be ruthless with reputation. The association in your mind is probably with a half-forgotten scandal and disgrace. You'd never heard of me, the once obscure novelist Parker Sparrow, until my name was publicly connected with his. To a knowing few, our names remain rigidly attached, like the two ends of a seesaw. His rise coincided with, though did not cause, my decline. Then his descent was my earthly triumph. I don't deny there was wrongdoing. I stole a life, and I don't intend to give it back. You may treat these few pages as a confession.

To make it fully, I must go back forty years, to a time when our lives happily and entirely overlapped, and seemed poised to run in parallel toward a shared future. We studied at the same university, read the same subject – English literature – published our first stories in student magazines with names like *Knife in Your Eye*. (But what names are like that?) We were ambitious. We wanted to be writers, famous writers, even great writers. We took holidays together and read each other's stories, gave generous, savagely honest comments, made love to each other's girlfriends, and, on a few occasions, tried to interest ourselves in a homoerotic affair. I'm fat and bald now, but then I had a head of curls and was slender. I liked to think I resembled Shelley. Jocelyn was tall, blond, muscular, with a firm jawline, the very image of the *Übermensch* Nazi. But he had no taste for politics at all. Our affair was simply bohemian posturing. We thought it made us fascinating. The truth was that we were each repelled by the sight of the other's penis. We did very little to or with each other, but we were happy to have people think we did a lot.

None of this got in the way of our literary friendship. I don't think we were properly competitive at the time. But, looking back, I'd say that initially I was the one who was ahead. I was the first to publish in a real, grownup literary magazine – *The North London Review*. At the end of our university career, I got a good first, Jocelyn got a second-class degree. We decided that such things were irrelevant, and so they turned out to be. We moved to London and took single rooms just a few streets away from each other in Brixton. I published my second story, so it was a relief when he published his first. We continued to meet regularly, get drunk, read each other's stuff, and we began to move in the same pleasantly downtrodden literary circles. We even began at roughly the same time to write reviews for the respectable national press.

Those two years after university were the height of our fraternal youth. We were growing up fast. We were both working on our first novels, and they had much in common: sex, mayhem, a touch of apocalypse, some violence, some fashionable despair, and very good jokes about all the things that can go wrong between a young man and a young woman. We were happy. Nothing stood in our way.

Then two things did. Jocelyn, without telling me, wrote a TV play. That sort of thing, I thought at the time, was well beneath us. We worshipped at the temple of literature. TV was mere entertainment, dross for the masses. The screenplay was immediately produced, starred two famous actors, was passionate about a good cause – homelessness or unemployment – that I had never heard Jocelyn mention. It was a success; he was talked about, noted. His first novel was anticipated. None of that would have mattered if I had not, at the same time, met Arabella, an English rose, ample, generous, calm, a funny girl who remains my wife even today. I'd had a dozen lovers before then, but I got no farther than Arabella. She laid on everything I needed by way of sex and friendship and adventure and variation. Such a passion was not enough in itself to stand between Jocelyn and me, or me and my ambitions. Far from it. Arabella's nature was copious, unjealous, all-embracing, and she liked Jocelyn from the start.

What changed was that we had a child, a boy named Matt, on whose first birthday Arabella and I were married. My Brixton room could not accommodate us for long. We moved farther south, deeper into the postal districts of southwest London, first to SW12, later to SW17. From there, one reached Charing Cross by a twenty-minute train ride, which itself began only after a twenty-five-minute walk through the suburbs. My freelance writing could not support us. I found a part-time teaching job in a local college. Arabella became pregnant again – she loved being pregnant. My college job turned full time just as my first novel was published. There was praise; there was mild damnation. Six weeks later, Jocelyn's first novel was out – an instant success. Though it didn't sell much more than mine (in those days, sales hardly mattered), his name already had a ring to it. There was a hunger for a new voice, and Jocelyn Tarbet sang more sweetly than I ever could.

His looks and his height (Nazi is unfair – let's say Bruce Chatwin, with Mick Jagger's scowl), his high turnover of interesting girlfriends, the beaten-up MGA sports car he drove fed his reputation. Was I envious? I don't think so. I was in love with three people – our children seemed to me divine beings. Everything they said or did fascinated me, and Arabella continued to fascinate me, too. She was soon pregnant again, and we moved north, to Nottingham. With teaching and family responsibilities, it took me five years to write my second novel. There was praise, a little more than last time; there was damnation, a little less than last time. No one but me remembered the last time.

By then, Jocelyn was publishing his third. The first had already been made into a movie starring Julie Christie. He'd had a divorce, a mews house in Notting Hill, many interviews on TV, many photographs in life-style magazines. He said hilarious, scathing things about the Prime Minister. He was becoming our generation's spokesman. But here's the astonishing thing: our friendship did not falter. Certainly, it became more intermittent. We were busy in our separate realms. We had to get the desk diaries out well in advance in order to see each other. Occasionally, he travelled up to see me and the family. (By the time of our fourth child, we had moved even farther north, to Durham.) But usually I was the one who travelled south to see him and his second wife, Joliet. They lived in a large Victorian house in Hampstead, right near the heath.

Mostly, we drank and talked and walked on the heath. If you'd been listening in, you would have heard nothing between us to suggest that he was the star and that my literary prospects were fading. He assumed that my opinions were as important as his; he never condescended. He even remembered my children's birthdays. I was always installed in the best guest room. Joliet was welcoming. Jocelyn invited friends around, who all seemed lively and pleasant. He cooked big meals. He and I were, as we often said, 'family'.

But, of course, there were differences that neither of us could ignore. My place in Durham was friendly enough, but child-trampled, crowded, cold in the winter. The chairs and carpets had been wrecked by a dog and two cats.

The kitchen was always full of laundry, because that was where the washing machine was. The house was afflicted with many ginger-coloured pine fittings that we never had time to paint or replace. There was rarely more than one bottle of wine in the house. The kids were fun, but they were chaotic and noisy. We lived on my modest salary and Arabella's part-time nursing. We had no savings, few luxuries. It was hard in my house to find a place to read a book. Or to find a book.

So it was a holiday of the senses to pitch up at Jocelyn and Joliet's for a weekend. The vast library, the coffee tables supporting that month's hardbacks, the expanses of dark polished oak floor, paintings, rugs, a grand piano, violin music on a stand, the banked towels in my bedroom, its awesome shower, the grownup hush that lay around the house, the sense of order and shine that only a daily cleaning lady can bestow. There was a garden with an ancient willow, a mossy Yorkstone terrace, a wide lawn, and high walls. And, more than all this, the place was pervaded by a spirit of open-mindedness, curiosity, tolerance, and a taste for comedy. How could I stay away?

I suppose I should confess to one solitary strain of dark sentiment, a theme of vague unease I never gave expression to. Honestly, it didn't trouble me that much. I'd written four novels in fifteen years – a heroic achievement, given my teaching load and hands-on fathering and lack of space. All four were out of print. I no longer had a publisher. I always sent a finished copy of my latest to my old friend with a warm dedication. He would thank me for it, but he never passed comment. I'm quite sure that after our Brixton days he never read a word of mine. He sent me early copies of his novels, too – nine to my four. I wrote him long appreciative letters about the first two or three, then I decided for the sake of our friendship's equilibrium to respond in kind. We no longer talked or wrote about each other's books – and that seemed fine.

So you find us past midlife, around the age of fifty. Jocelyn was a national treasure, and I – well, it was wrong to think in terms of failure. All my children had processed or were processing through university, I still played a decent game of tennis, my marriage, after a few creaks and groans and two explosive crises, was holding together, and the rumour was that I'd be a full professor within the year. I was also writing my fifth novel – but that was not going awfully well.

And now I come to the core of this story, the seesaw's crucial tilt. It was early July and I headed from Durham to Hampstead, as I often did straight after marking finals papers. As usual, I was in a state of pleasant exhaustion. But this was not the usual visit. The following day, Jocelyn and Joliet were going to Orvieto for the week and I was going to house-sit – feed their cat, water the plants, and make use of the space and the silence to work on the meandering fifty-eight pages of my novel.

When I arrived, Jocelyn was out running errands and Joliet made me welcome. She was a specialist in X-ray crystallography at Imperial College, a beautiful, sleek woman with a warm, low voice and an intimate manner. We sat drinking tea in the garden, swapping news. And then, with a pause and an introductory frown, as if she had planned the moment, she told me about Jocelyn, how things were not going so well with his work. He'd finished a final draft of a novel and was depressed. It had failed to measure up to his ambitions, for this was supposed to be an important book. He was miserable. He didn't think he could improve it; nor could he bring himself to destroy it. It was she who'd suggested they take a short holiday and walk the dusty white tracks around Orvieto. He needed rest and distance from his pages. While we sat in the shade of the enormous willow, she told me how downcast Jocelyn had been. She had offered to read the novel, but he had refused – reasonably enough, for she's not really a literary sort of person.

When she'd finished, I said airily, 'I'm sure he can rescue it if he can just get away for a while.'

They set off the following morning. I fed the cat, made myself a second coffee, then spread my pages on a desk in the guest room. The huge, dustless house was silent. But my thoughts kept returning to Joliet's story. It seemed so odd that my ever-successful friend should have a crisis of confidence. The fact interested me; it even cheered me a little. After an hour, without taking any sort of decision, I wandered toward Jocelyn's study. Locked. In the same open-minded spirit, I wandered into the master bedroom. I remembered from our Brixton days where he used to keep his marijuana. It didn't take me long to find the key, at the back of his sock drawer.

You won't believe this, but I had no plan. I just wanted to see.

On his desk, a huge old electric typewriter hummed – he had forgotten to turn it off. He was among the many word-processing holdouts in the literary world. The typescript was right there, in a neatly squared-off pile, six hundred pages – long, but not vast. The title was *The Tumult,* and underneath I saw, in pencil, 'fifth draft', followed by the previous week's date.

I sat down in my old friend's study chair and began to read. Two hours later, in a kind of dream, I took a break, went into the garden for ten minutes, then decided that I should get on with my own wretched attempt. Instead, I found myself drawn back to Jocelyn's desk. I hesitated by it, then I sat down. I read all day, paused for supper, read until late, woke early, and finished at lunchtime.

It was magnificent. By far his best. Better than any contemporary novel I remembered reading. If I say it was Tolstoyan in its ambition, it was also modernist, Proustian, Joycean in execution. It had moments of joy and terrible grief. His prose sang more beautifully than ever. It was worldly; it gave us London; it gave us the twentieth century. The depictions of the five central characters overwhelmed me with their truth, their brightness. I felt I'd always known such people. Sometimes they seemed too close, too real. The end – matter of fifty pages – was symphonic in its slow, unfolding grandeur, sorrowful, understated, honest, and I was in tears. Not only for the plight of the characters but for the whole superb conception, its understanding of love and regret and fate, and its warm sympathy for the frailty of human nature.

I stood up from the desk. Distractedly, I watched a battered-looking thrush hopping backward and forward across the lawn in search of a worm. I do not say this in my defence, but, again, I was empty of schemes. I experienced only the glow of an extraordinary reading experience, a form of profound gratitude familiar to all who love literature.

I say I had no plan, but I knew what I would do next. I simply enacted what others might only have thought. I moved like a zombie, distancing myself from my own actions. I also told myself that I was just taking precautions, that most likely nothing would come of what I was doing. This formulation was a cushion, a vital protection. Looking back now, I wonder if I was prompted by rumours of the Lee Israel forgeries, or by Borges's *Pierre Menard*, or Calvino's *If on a Winter's*

Night a Traveller. Or an episode in a novel I'd read the year before, *The Information,* by Martin Amis. I'm reliably informed that Amis himself derived that episode from an evening of drinking with another novelist, the one (memory fails me) with the Scottish name and the English attitude. I heard that the two friends entertained themselves by dreaming up all the ways one writer might ruin the life of another. But this was different. It may sound improbable, given what followed, but on that morning I had no thoughts of causing Jocelyn any harm. I was thinking only of myself. I had ambitions.

I carried the pages into the kitchen and tipped them into a plastic bag. I took a taxi across London to an obscure street where I knew there was a photocopying shop. I came back, returned the original to Jocelyn's desk, locked the study, wiped my prints off the key, returned it to his sock drawer.

Back in the guest room, I took from my briefcase one of my empty notebooks – I'm always given them for Christmas – and got to work, serious work. I started making extended notes for the novel I had just read. The first entry I dated two years in the past. I deliberately strayed from the subject several times, pursued irrelevant ideas, but kept coming back to the central line of the story. I wrote at speed for three days, filling two notebooks, sketching out scenes. I found new names for the characters, altered aspects of their pasts, their surroundings, details of their faces. I managed to work in some minor themes from my previous novels. I even quoted myself. I thought New York would serve for London. Then I realised that I could never bring any city to life the way Jocelyn had, so I returned to London. I worked hard and I began to feel that I was being truly creative. This was, after all, going to be my novel as well as his.

In the remainder of my stay, I typed out my first three chapters. A few hours before they were due to return, I left Jocelyn and Joliet a note explaining that I had to return north for an examiners' meeting. You might think that I was being a coward, that I couldn't face the man I was stealing from. But it wasn't like that. I wanted to get away and keep working. I already had twenty thousand words and I was desperate to press on.

At home, I told Arabella, truthfully, that my week had been a complete success. I was onto something important. I wanted to spend the summer holidays developing it. I worked through the rest of July. In mid-August, I printed out my first draft and made a bonfire in the garden of my photocopy. I made a mass of corrections on the pages, typed in my marks, and in early September the new draft was ready. Let's face it, the novel was still Jocelyn's. There were brilliant passages of his that I left almost intact. But there was enough of my own writing there to allow me a sense of proud possession. I had sprinkled the pages with the dust of my identity. I'd even included a reference to my first novel, which one of the characters is seen reading – on a beach.

My publisher, in one of those savage clear-outs of the so-called 'mid-list', had, with 'profound regret', let me go. I was contractually free. Rather than self-publish on the Internet, I chose to go with an old-fashioned vanity press called Gorgeous Books. It was a dismayingly rapid process. Within a week, I had in my hands an early copy of *The Dance She Refused.* The cover was purple, with gold embossed letters in flowery copperplate, and the pages were faintly perfumed. I inscribed one and sent it by registered post to my dear friend. I knew he would never read it.

All this was achieved before I resumed teaching, in late September. During the autumn, in my free time, I sent the book around to friends, to bookshops, newspapers, always making sure to enclose a hopeful little note. I gave copies to charity shops in the hope of gaining a humble circulation. I slipped copies onto the shelves of secondhand-book shops. I heard by e-mail from Jocelyn that he had put *The Tumult* aside and was working on something new. I knew now that I had nothing to do but wait – and hope.

Two years passed. I made my usual visits to Hampstead, and we avoided, as we often did, talk of our own work. In that period, I did not hear from a single person, apart from my wife, on the subject of *The Dance She Refused.* Arabella was swept away by it, indignant, then furious, that it was ignored. She told me that my famous friend should be doing something to help. I told her calmly that it was a matter of pride not to ask him. On trips to London, I distributed more copies of *The Dance* in secondhand-book stores. By Christmas, almost four hundred copies were out in the world.

Three years separated the appearance of *The Dance She Refused* and *The Tumult.* As I'd expected, friends had told Jocelyn that he'd written his best and he must publish. When he did, the press was also, as I'd expected, a sweet chorus of songbirds in fluting ecstasy. I hung back in case the process I had set in train found its own momentum. But since no one had read my perfumed version, nothing could happen. I was obliged to give the matter a shove. I sent my creation in a plain envelope to a bitter, gossipy critic on the London *Evening Standard.* My unsigned note said, in Courier sixteen point, 'Does this remind you of a highly successful novel published last month?'

Much of the rest you will know. It was the perfect story. A wild storm surged through my house and Jocelyn's. All the correct ingredients. A wretched villain, a quiet hero. A national treasure knocked flying from his pedestal, dishonest fingers deep in the till, an old friend down on his luck, betrayed, whole passages lifted, whole conception stolen, characters, too, no plausible explanation from the guilty man, whose friends now understood his reluctance to publish, tens of thousands of copies of *The Tumult* removed from the shops and pulped. And the old friend? Nobly refused to condemn, unavailable for interviews – and, of course, a genius revealed, best book in years, a modern classic, a mild man loved by his students and colleagues, dumped by his publisher, books out of print. Then a scramble to procure the rights, all the rights, to the backlist as well as *Dance*, agents and auctions involved, film rights and movie people involved. Then the prizes – Booker, Whitbread, Medici, Critics' Circle, in one long noisy banquet. Copies of the Gorgeous edition selling for five thousand pounds on AbeBooks. Then, as the dust settled, and with my book still 'flying' off the shelves, thoughtful articles on the nature of literary kleptomania, the strange compulsion to be caught, and acts of artistic self-destruction in late middle age.

In e-mails and phone calls with Jocelyn, I was cool. I sounded offended without saying so, keen to break off, at least for now. When he told me how baffled he was, I cleared my throat, paused, then reminded him of the copy I'd sent. How else could it have happened? Finally, I gave one interview, to a California magazine. It became the authoritative version, picked up by the rest of the press. I allowed the journalist access to my notebooks, rejection slips and letters, copies of the hopeful notes I had attached to my purple copies. He saw my crowded circumstances; he met my cheerful, charming wife and friendly children. He wrote of my dedication to the high cause of my art, my quiet reluctance to criticise an old friend, of the indignities of vanity publishing suffered without complaint, the rediscovery of a brilliant backlist comparable to the John Williams phenomenon. Courtesy of the American weekly, I became a saint.

In my private life, all predictable enough. Eventually, we bought a big old house on the edge of a village three miles out of Durham. A stately river runs through the grounds. At my sixtieth birthday, two grandchildren were in attendance. The year before, I'd accepted a knighthood. I remain a saint, an exceedingly rich saint, and I'm close to becoming a national treasure. My sixth novel didn't do so well with the critics, though the sales were Rowlingesque. I think I might stop writing. I don't think anyone would mind.

And Jocelyn? Also predictable. No one in publishing would touch him; nor would the readers. He sold his house, moved to Brixton, our old stamping ground, where, he says, he feels more comfortable anyway. He teaches creative-writing night classes in Lewisham. It pleases me that Joliet stuck by him. And there are no issues between us. We remain close. I've forgiven him completely. He often comes to stay and always has the best guest room, facing the river, where he likes to fish for trout and row for miles. Sometimes Joliet comes up with him. They like our old university friends, who are kind and tolerant. Often, he cooks for us all. I think he's grateful that I've dropped any hint of an accusation that he ever looked inside that purple scented edition.

Sometimes, late at night, when he and I are sitting by the fire (it's a vast fireplace), drinking and raking over this curious episode, this disaster, he tells me again his own theory, which he's been refining over the years. Our lives, he says, were always entwined. We talked over everything a thousand times, read the same books, lived through and shared so much, and in some curious way our thoughts, our imaginations fused to such an extent that we ended up writing the same novel, more or less.

I cross the room with a bottle of decent Pomerol to refill his glass. It's just a theory, I tell him, but it's a good-hearted theory, a loving idea that celebrates the very essence of our long, unbreakable friendship. We're family.

We raise our glasses.

Cheers!